Pakenham Beatty, Robert Bridges

Songs Of Adieu

Pakenham Beatty, Robert Bridges

Songs Of Adieu

ISBN/EAN: 9783741113888

Manufactured in Europe, USA, Canada, Australia, Japa

Cover: Foto ©Andreas Hilbeck / pixelio.de

Manufactured and distributed by brebook publishing software
(www.brebook.com)

Pakenham Beatty, Robert Bridges

Songs Of Adieu

The Bibelot Series.

SONGS OF ADIEU.

MUSIC, *when soft voices die,*
Vibrates in the memory;
Odours, *when sweet violets sicken,*
Live within the sense they quicken;

Rose leaves, when the rose is dead,
Are heaped for the beloved's bed;
And so thy thoughts, when thou art gone,
Love itself shall slumber on.

PERCY BYSSHE SHELLEY.

SONGS OF ADIEU: A
LITTLE BOOK of

" Finale and

Farewell ."

Mais où sont les neiges d'antan!

Printed for Thomas B. Mosher
and Published by him at
37 Exchange Street, Portland,
Maine. Mdcccxciij.

CONTENTS.

CONTENTS.

CONTENTS.

Farewell the song says only, being
  A star whose race is run,
Farewell the soul says never, seeing
  The sun.

A. C. SWINBURNE.

SONGS OF ADIEU.

*From "The Shorter Poems" of
Robert Bridges, (London, 1890.)*

I HAVE LOVED FLOWERS THAT FADE.

*I HAVE loved flowers that fade;
    Within whose magic tents
Rich hues have marriage made
    With sweet unmemoried scents:
A honeymoon delight,—
A joy of love at sight,
That ages in an hour :—
My song be like a flower !*

*I have loved airs, that die
    Before their charm is writ
Along a liquid sky
    Trembling to welcome it.
Notes, that with pulse of fire
Proclaim the spirit's desire,
Then die, and are nowhere :—
My song be like an air !*

*Die, song, die like a breath,
    And wither as a bloom :
Fear not a flowery death,
    Dread not an airy tomb !
Fly with delight, fly hence !
'Twas thine love's tender sense
To feast, now on thy bier
Beauty shall shed a tear.*

From "Poems" by Owen Meredith,
(Boston, 1872.)

AUX ITALIENS.

A<small>T</small> *Paris it was, at the Opera there;—*
  And she look'd like a queen in a book that night,
With the wreath of pearl in her raven hair,
  And the brooch on her breast, so bright.

Of all the operas that Verdi wrote,
  The best, to my taste, is the Trovatore:
And Mario can soothe with a tenor note
  The souls in Purgatory.

The moon on the tower slept soft as snow:
  And who was not thrill'd in the strangest way,
As we heard him sing, while the gas burn'd low,
  "Non ti scordar di me?"

The Emperor there, in his box of state,
  Look'd grave, as if he had just then seen
The red flag wave from the city-gate,
  Where his eagles in bronze had been.

The Empress, too, had a tear in her eye.
  You'd have said that her fancy had gone back again,
For one moment, under the old blue sky,
  To the old glad life in Spain.

xii

Well! there in our front-row box we sat,
  Together, my bride-betroth'd and I:
My gaze was fix'd on my opera-hat,
  And hers on the stage hard by.

And both were silent, and both were sad.
  Like a queen, she lean'd on her full white arm,
With that regal, indolent air she had;
  So confident of her charm!

I have not a doubt she was thinking then
  Of her former lord, good soul that he was!
Who died the richest, and roundest of men,
  The Marquis of Carabas.

I hope that, to get to the kingdom of heaven,
  Thro' a needle's eye he had not to pass.
I wish him well, for the jointure given
  To my lady of Carabas.

Meanwhile, I was thinking of my first love,
  As I had not been thinking of aught for years,
Till over my eyes there began to move
  Something that felt like tears.

I thought of the dress that she wore last time,
  When we stood, 'neath the cypress trees, together,
In that lost land, in that soft clime,
  In the crimson evening weather:

Of that muslin dress (for the eve was hot)
  And her warm white neck in its golden chain,
And her full, soft hair, just tied in a knot,
  And falling loose again:

And the jasmin-flower in her fair young breast :
  (O the faint, sweet smell of that jasmin-flower !)
And the one bird singing alone to his nest :
  And the one star over the tower.

I thought of our little quarrels and strife ;
  And the letter that brought me back my ring.
And it all seem'd then, in the waste of life,
  Such a very little thing !

For I thought of her grave below the hill,
  Which the sentinel cypress-tree stands over.
And I thought . . . "were she only living still,
  How I could forgive her, and love her !"

And I swear, as I thought of her thus, in that hour,
  And of how, after all, old things were best,
That I smelt the smell of that jasmin-flower,
  Which she used to wear in her breast.

It smelt so faint, and it smelt so sweet,
  It made me creep, and it made me cold !
Like the scent that steals from the crumbling sheet
  Where a mummy is half unroll'd.

And I turn'd, and look'd. She was sitting there
  In a dim box, over the stage ; and drest
In that muslin dress, with that full soft hair,
  And that jasmin in her breast !

I was here : and she was there :
  And the glittering horseshoe curved between :—
From my bride-betroth'd, with her raven hair,
  And her sumptuous, scornful mien.

xiv

To my early love, with her eyes downcast,
  And over her primrose face the shade,
(In short from the Future back to the Past)
  There was but a step to be made.

To my early love from my future bride
  One moment I look'd.   Then I stole to the door ;
I travers'd the passage ; and down at her side,
  I was sitting, a moment more.

My thinking of her, or the music's strain,
  Or something which never will be exprest,
Had brought her back from the grave again, .
  With the jasmin in her breast.

She is not dead, and she is not wed!
  But she loves me now, and she loved me then!
And the very first word that her sweet lips said,
  My heart grew youthful again.

The Marchioness there, of Carabas,
  She is wealthy, and young, and handsome still,
And but for her . . . well, we'll let that pass,
  She may marry whomever she will.

But I will marry my own first love,
  With her primrose face : for old things are best
And the flower in her bosom, I prize it above
  The brooch in my lady's breast.

The world is fill'd with folly and sin,
  And Love must cling where it can, I say :
For Beauty is easy enough to win ;
  But one isn't loved every day.

XV

And I think, in the lives of most women and men,
  There's a moment when all would go smooth and even,
If only the dead could find out when
  To come back, and be forgiven.

But O the smell of that jasmin flower!
  And O that music! and O the way
That voice rang out from the donjon tower
  Non ti scordar di me,
    Non ti scordar di me!

From "Old-World Idylls" by Austin Dobson, (London, 1885.)

POT-POURRI.

"SI JEUNESSE SAVAIT?—"

I PLUNGE *my hand among the leaves:*
(An alien touch but dust perceives,
   Nought else supposes ;)
For me those fragrant ruins raise
Clear memory of the vanished days
   When they were roses.

"If youth but knew!" · Ah, "if," in truth—
I can recall with what gay youth,
   To what light chorus,
Unsobered yet by time or change,
We roamed the many-gabled Grange,
   All life before us ;

Braved the old clock-tower's dust and damp
To catch the dim Arthurian camp
   In misty distance ;
Peered at the still-room's sacred stores,
Or rapped at walls for sliding doors
   Of feigned existence.

What need had we for thoughts or cares !
The hot sun parched the old parterres
   And "flowerful closes";
We roused the rooks with rounds and glees,
Played hide-and-seek behind the trees,—
   Then plucked these roses.

Louise was one—light, glib Louise,
So freshly freed from school decrees
        You scarce could stop her;
And Bell, the Beauty, unsurprised
At fallen locks that scandalized
        Our dear "Miss Proper":—

Shy Ruth, all heart and tenderness,
Who wept—like Chaucer's Prioress,
        When Dash was smitten;
Who blushed before the mildest men,
Yet waxed a very Corday when
        You teased her kitten.

I loved them all.   Bell first and best;
Louise the next—for days of jest
        Or madcap masking;
And Ruth, I thought,—why, failing these,
When my High-Mightiness should please,
        She'd come for asking.

        .   .   .   .   .

Louise was grave when last we met;
Bell's beauty, like a sun, has set;
        And Ruth, Heaven bless her,
Ruth that I wooed,—and wooed in vain,
Has gone where neither grief nor pain
        Can now distress her.

From "*A London Plane-Tree and Other Verse*" by *Amy Levy*, (*London, 1889.*)

IN THE MILE END ROAD.

How *like her! But 'tis she herself,*
  Comes up the crowded street,
How little did I think, the morn,
  My only love to meet!

Whose else that motion and that mien?
  Whose else that airy tread?
For one strange moment I forgot
  My only love was dead.

From "Music and Moonlight" by Arthur O'Shaughnessy, (London, 1874.)

SONG.

I MADE *another garden, yea,*
  For my new love;
I left the dead rose where it lay,
  And set the new above.
Why did the summer not begin?
  Why did my heart not haste?
My old love came and walked therein,
  And laid the garden waste.

She entered with her weary smile,
  Just as of old;
She looked around a little while,
  And shivered at the cold.
Her passing touch was death to all,
  Her passing look a blight:
She made the white rose-petals fall,
  And turned the red rose white.

Her pale robe, clinging to the grass,
  Seemed like a snake
That bit the grass and ground, alas!
  And a sad trail did make.
She went up slowly to the gate;
  And there, just as of yore,
She turned back at the last to wait,
  And say farewell once more.

EHEU FUGACES!

L IGHT *and soft they flutter down,*
   Faded gauds from Autumn's crown:
      Still they fall
With a slow, pathetic grace,
Touching now my hands, my face;
      Now—the wall.

"Ohne Hast und ohne Rast,"
Chill and grey the years have passed,
      Ay de mi!
By this old red orchard wall
One fair face I still recall—
      Almost see!

Ah, that still September day!
Bravely seemed the world and gay
      To us then.
Then, we stood together here;
Now, the leaves fall, brown and sere,
      Once again.

Worn and weary, old and grey,
Altered seems the world to-day—
      Mine the blame;
For I see with time-dimmed eyes,
Though the kind autumnal skies
      Smile the same.

Pure as winsome, fair as true;
Hard the fate that lost me you—
        Oh, my dear!
Still I see you leaning there,
With the dead leaves on your hair,
        Far, yet near.

My Neæra—vainly sought!
What to you has Fortune brought
        Since we met?
Love or hatred, doul or glee?
But her only gift to me
        Is—regret!

From "Primavera: Poems by Four Authors,"
(Stephen Phillips), (Oxford, 1890.)

A DREAM.

MY *dead love came to me, and said,*
  'God gives me one hour's rest,
To spend with thee on earth again:
  How shall we spend it best'?

'Why, as of old,' I said; and so
  We quarrell'd, as of old:
But, when I turned to make my peace,
  That one short hour was told.

From "Spretæ Carmina Musæ" by
Pakenham Beatty, (London, 1893.)

"IF MAY FORGETS NOT APRIL'S FLOWERS."

IF *May forgets not April's flowers,*
  June will—
Even hearts as passionate as ours
    Grow still!

July forgets what birds and flowers
  June had—
Even hearts whose joy is deep as ours
    Grow sad!

The pale leaves hear not what the flowers
  Heard told—
Even hearts as passionate as ours
    Grow cold!

From "New and Old" by John Addington
Symonds, (London. 1880.)

FAREWELL.

THOU goest: to what distant place
    Wilt thou thy sunlight carry?
I stay with cold and clouded face:
    How long am I to tarry?
Where'er thou goest, morn will be;
Thou leavest night and gloom to me. *

The night and gloom I can but take;
    I do not grudge thy splendour:
Bid souls of eager men awake;
    Be kind and bright and tender.
Give day to other worlds; for me
It must suffice to dream of thee.

From "Poems" by Alice Meynell
(London, 1893.)

REGRETS.

As, when the seaward ebbing tide doth pour
  Out by the low sand spaces,
The parting waves slip back to clasp the shore
  With lingering embraces,—

So in the tide of life that carries me
  From where thy true heart dwells,
Waves of my thoughts and memories turn to thee
  With lessening farewells;

Waving of hands; dreams, when the day forgets;
  A care half lost in cares;
The saddest of my verses; dim regrets;
  Thy name among my prayers.

I would the day might come, so waited for,
  So patiently besought,
When I, returning, should fill up once more
  Thy desolated thought;

And fill thy loneliness that lies apart
  In still, persistent pain.
Shall I content thee, O thou broken heart,
  As the tide comes again,

And brims the little sea-shore lakes, and sets
  Seaweeds afloat, and fills
The silent pools, rivers and rivulets
  Among the inland hills?

xxvi

From "Grass of Parnassus" by
Andrew Lang, (London, 1888.)

A DREAM.

WHY will you haunt my sleep?
  You know it may not be,
The grave is wide and deep,
  That sunders you and me ;
In bitter dreams we reap
  The sorrow we have sown,
And I would I were asleep,
  Forgotten and alone !

We knew and did not know,
  We saw and did not see,
The nets that long ago
  Fate wove for you and me ;
The cruel nets that keep
  The birds that sob and moan,
And I would we were asleep,
  Forgotten and alone !

. . .

From "An Italian Garden" by A. Mary
F. Robinson, (London, 1886.)

CASTELLO.

THE *Triton in the Ilex-wood*
  Is lonely at Castello.
The snow is on him like a hood,
  The fountain-reeds are yellow.

But never Triton sorrowed yet
  For weather chill or mellow;
He mourns, my Dear, that you forget
  The gardens of Castello!

*From "Silhouettes" by Arthur
Symons, (London, 1892.)*

SOUVENIR.

How you haunt me with your eyes!
  Still that questioning persistence,
  Sad and sweet, across the distance
  Of the days of love and laughter,
Those old days of love and lies.

  Not reproaching, not reproving,
  Only, always, questioning,
  Those divinest eyes can bring
  Memories of certain summers,—
Nights of dreaming, days of loving,—

  When I loved you, when your kiss
  (Shyer than a bird to capture)
  Lit a sudden heaven of rapture;
  When we neither dreamt that either
Could grow old in heart like this.

  Do you still, in love's December,
  Still remember, still regret
  That sweet unavailing debt?
  Ah, you haunt me, to remind me
You remember, I forget!

From "Songs in Exile" by H. E. Clarke,
(London, 1879.)

AGE.

ALL the strong spells of Passion slowly breaking,
    Its chains undone;
A troubled sleep that dreams to peaceful waking,
    A haven won.

A fire burnt out unto the last dead ember,
    Left black and cold;
A fiery August unto still September
    Yielding her gold.

A dawn serene the windy midnight over,
    The darkness past;
Now, with no clouds nor mists her face to cover,
    The Day at last.

Thou hast thy prayed-for peace, O soul, and quiet
    From storm and strife;—
Now yearn forever for the noise and riot
    That made thy Life.

XXX

From "A Book of Verses" by William
Ernest Henley, (London, 1888.)

CROSSES AND TROUBLES.

CROSSES and troubles a-many have proved me.
One or two women (God bless them!) have loved me.
I have worked and dreamed, and I've talked at will,
Of art and drink I have had my fill.
I've comforted here, and I've succoured there.
I've faced my foes, and I've backed my friends.
I've blundered, and sometimes made amends.
I have prayed for light, and I've known despair.
Now I look before, as I look behind,
Come storm, come shine, whatever befall,
With a grateful heart and a constant mind,
For the end, I know, is the best of all.

From "Wordsworth's Grave and Other Poems"
by William Watson, (London, 1890.)

WHEN BIRDS WERE SONGLESS.

WHEN *birds were songless on the bough*
 I heard thee sing.
The world was full of winter, thou
 Wert full of spring.

To-day the world's heart feels anew
 The vernal thrill,
And thine beneath the rueful yew
 Is wintry chill.

From "Selections from the Verse of
Augusta Webster, (London, 1893.)

"THE COMMON FATE OF ALL THINGS RARE."

So strange it is to me
  Beauty should perishably find its close
That sometimes, looking on a girl's gold hair,
That sometimes, looking on a perfect rose,
  I see in it the loss that is to be
And am made mournful by its being fair.

  It cannot be but pain,
Wondering how showed some loveliest face of yore,
  To think "'Tis gone that was so exquisite;
Delight went from the world that comes no more—
  Some other but not ever that again.
Dead; and we could have been so glad of it!

  But there's a sadder sense
When loveliness is lapsing to decay,
  The flower grown sere that was so sweet a prize,
The face that made men's sunshine fallen and grey.
  Oh loss, that fair should fade ere it goes hence,
Should change forgotten in Time's dusk disguise!

  Saddest of all is this,
The while one's eyes gaze happy even to tears,
  To have it in one's heart "And this fair thing,
Except it die too early, nears and nears
  A time that shall transform it all amiss,
The time of warping and blurred withering."

  Saddest of all is this:
Yet how not sometimes spoil delight with thought,
  Measuring the beauty by the loss for aye,
Since its completing points its road to Nought,
  Since having been lurks waiting for what is?
Woe's me, that fair is fair for but its day!

*From "Harlequinade: a Book of Verses" by
Justin Huntly McCarthy, (London, 1890.)*

GOOD-NIGHT.

S WEETHEART, *here's a fair good-night
    To the golden year that's flying,
Fading as an emperor might,
Soothed by laughter to delight,
    On a throne of purple lying;
While before his swimming sight
Floating tresses, bodies white,
Sound of song and dance invite
    To departure without sighing.*

*Peace be with the year that's fled,
    Pleasure with the year to follow:
May the roses' deepest red
Give their garlands for your head!
    May your life be like the swallow,
Always by the sunlight led!
May your lightest wish be sped!
May you never dream or dread
    That the merry world is hollow!*

From Silhouettes" by Arthur Symons, (London, 1892.)

AFTER LOVE.

O TO *part now, and, parting now,*
 Never to meet again;
To have done forever, I and thou,
 With joy, and so with pain.

It is too hard, too hard to meet
 As friends, and love no more;
Those other meetings were too sweet
 That went before.

And I would have, now love is over,
 An end to all, an end:
I cannot, having been your lover,
 Stoop to become your friend!

From "*Love Lies Bleeding*" (*Anonymous*)
(*Oxford, 1891.*)

A SONG OF FAREWELL.

Fade, *vision bright!*
   What clinging bands can stay thee?
Die, dream of light!
   What clasping bands can pray thee?
Farewell, delight!
   I have no more to say thee.

The gold was gold,
   The little while it lasted;
The dream was true,
   Although its joy be blasted;
That hour was mine,
   Although so swift it hasted.

ı

From "Poems, Dramatic and Lyrical"
by Lord De Tabley, (London, 1893.)

THE CHURCHYARD ON THE SANDS.

M*Y Love lies in the gates of foam,*
  The last dear wreck of shore;
The naked sea-marsh binds her home,
  The sand her chamber door.

The gray gull flaps the written stones,
  The ox-birds chase the tide;
And near that narrow field of bones
  Great ships at anchor ride.

Black piers with crust of dripping green,
  One foreland, like a band,
O'er intervals of grass between
  Dim lonely dunes of sand.

A church of silent weathered looks,
  A breezy reddish tower,
A yard whose mounded resting-nooks
  Are tinged with sorrel flower.

In peace the swallow's eggs are laid
  Along the belfry walls;
The tempest does not reach her shade,
  The rain her silent halls.

But sails are sweet in summer sky,
  The lark throws down a lay;
The long salt levels steam and dry,
  The cloud-heart melts away.

But patches of the sea-pink shine,
  The pied crows poise and come;
The mallow hangs, the bindweeds twine,
  Where her sweet lips are dumb.

The passion of the wave is mute;
  No sound or ocean shock;
No music save the trilling flute
  That marks the curlew flock.

But yonder when the wind is keen,
  And rainy air is clear,
The merchant city's spires are seen,
  The toil of men grows near.

Along the coast-way grind the wheels
  Of endless carts of coal;
And on the sides of giant keels
  The shipyard hammers roll.

The world creeps here upon the shout,
  And stirs my heart in pain;
The mist descends and blots it out,
  And I am strong again.

Strong and alone, my dove, with thee;
  And, tho' mine eyes be wet,
There's nothing in the world to me
  So dear as my regret.

I would not change my sorrow, sweet,
    For others' nuptial hours;
I love the daisies at thy feet
    More than their orange flowers.

My hand alone shall tend thy tomb
    From leaf-bud to leaf-fall,
And wreathe around each season's bloom
    Till autumn ruins all.

Let snowdrops, early in the year,
    Droop o'er her silent breast;
And bid the later cowslip rear
    The amber of its crest.

Come hither, linnets tufted-red,
    Drift by, O wailing tern;
Set pure vale lilies at her head,
    At her feet lady-fern.

Grow, samphire, at the tidal brink,
    Wave, pansies of the shore,
To whisper how alone I think
    Of her forevermore.

Bring blue sea-hollies thorny, keen,
    Long lavender in flower;
Gray wormwood like a hoary queen,
    Stanch mullein like a tower.

O sea-wall mounded long and low,
    Let iron bounds be thine;
Nor let the salt wave overflow
    That breast I held divine.

Nor float its sea-weed to her hair,
  Nor dim her eyes with sands:
No fluted cockle burrow where
  Sleep folds her patient hands.

Tho' thy crest feel the wild sea's breath,
  Tho' tide-weight tear thy root,
Oh, guard the treasure-house, where Death
  Has bound my darling mute.

Tho' cold her pale lips to reward
  With love's own mysteries,
Ah, rob no daisy from her sward,
  Rough gale of eastern seas!

Ah, render sere no silken bent,
  That by her head-stone waves;
Let noon and golden summer blent
  Pervade these ocean graves.

And, ah, dear heart, in thy still nest,
  Resign this earth of woes,
Forget the ardours of the west,
  Neglect the morning glows.

Sleep, and forget all things but one
  Heard in each wave of sea,—
How lonely all the years will run
  Until I rest by thee.

From "Selections from the Verse of Augusta
Webster" (London, 1893.)

FAREWELL.

FAREWELL: *we two shall still meet day by day,*
   Live side by side:
But nevermore shall heart respond to heart.
   Two stranger boats can drift adown one tide,
Two branches on one stem grow green apart.
   Farewell, I say.

Farewell: chance travellers, as the path they tread,
   Change words and smile,
And share their travellers' fortunes, friend with friend,
   And yet are foreign in their thoughts the while,
Several, alone, save that one way they wend.
   Farewell; 'tis said.

Farewell: ever the bitter asphodel
   Outlives love's rose;
The fruit and blossom of the dead for us.
   Ah, answer me, should this have been the close,
To be together and be sundered thus?
   But yet, farewell.

*From "Diversi Colores" by Herbert
P. Horne, (London, 1891.)*

NEC VIOLAE SEMPER, NEC HIANTIA
LILIA FLORENT;
ET RIGET AMISSA SPINA RELICTA ROSA.

WHY are you fair? Is it because we know,
  Your beauty stays but for another hour?
Why are you sweet? Is it because you show,
  Even in the bud the blasting of the flower?
    Is it that we,
      Already in the mind,
    Too surely see
      The thoughtless, ruthless, hurry of the wind
    Scatter the petals of this perfect rose?

Why are you sad? Is it because our kisses,
  That were so sweet in kissing, now are past?
But are not all things swift to pass as this is,
  Which we desire to last?
Being too happy, we may not abide
  Within the happiness, that we possess;
But needs are swept on by the ceaseless tide
  Of Life's unwisdom, and of our distress:
As if, to all this crowd of ecstasies,
    The present close
  Were beauty faded, and deceivèd trust;
Locks, that no hands may braid; dull lifeless eyes,
  Eyes, that have wept their lustre into dust.
    Who knows?

From "Lyrics" by A. Mary F.
Robinson, (London, 1891.)

THE DEAD FRIEND.

I.

WHEN *you were alive, at least,*
  There were days I never met you.
In the study, at the feast,
  By the hearth, I could forget you.

Moods there were of many days
  When, methinks, I did not mind you.
Now, oh now, in any place
  Wheresoe'er I go, I find you!

You . . . . but how profoundly changed,
  O you dear-belov'd dead woman!
Made mysterious and estranged,
  All-pervading, superhuman.

Ah! to meet you as of yore,
  Kind, alert, and quick to laughter:
You, the friend I loved Before;
  Not this tragic friend of After.

II.

The house was empty where you came no more;
  I sat in awe and dread;
When, lo! I heard a hand that shook the door,
  And knew it was the Dead.

One moment—ah!—the anguish took my side,
  The fainting of the will.
"God of the living, leave me not"! I cried,
  And all my flesh grew chill.

One moment; then I opened wide my heart
  And open flung the door:
"What matter whence thou comest, what thou art?
  Come to me"! . . . . Never more.

III.

They lie at peace, the darkness fills
  The hollow of their empty gaze.
The dust falls in their ears and stills
  The echo of our fruitless days;

The earth takes back their baser part;
  The brain no longer bounds the dream;
The broken vial of the heart
  Lets out its passion in a stream.

And in this silence that they have
  One inner vision grows more bright;
The Dead remember in the grave
  As I remember here to-night.

From "A Lost Epic" by William
Canton, (London, 1887.)

TWO LIVES.

A MONG *the lonely hills they played;*
  No other bairns they ever knew;
A little lad, a little maid,
  In sweet companionship they grew.

  They played among the ferns and rocks
    A childish comedy of life—
  Kept house and milked the crimson docks,
    And called each other man and wife.

  They went to school; they used to go
    With arms about each other laid;
  Their flaxen heads, in rain or snow,
    Were sheltered by a single plaid.

  And so—and so it came to pass
    They loved each other ere they knew;
  His heart was like a blade o' grass,
    And hers was like its drap o' dew.

  The years went by; the changeful years
    Brought larger life and toil for life;
  They parted in the dusk with tears—
    They called each other man and wife.

  They married—she another man,
    And he in time another maid;
  The story ends as it began;—
    Among the lonely hills—they played!

xlv

From "The Century Guild Hobby Horse,"
1891, by Ernest Dowson."

"NON SUM QUALIS ERAM BONAE SUB REGNO CYNARAE."

LAST night, ah! yesternight, betwixt her lips and mine,
There fell thy shadow, Cynara! thy breath was shed
Upon my soul, between the kisses and the wine:
And I was desolate, and sick of an old passion:
Yea! I was desolate and bowed my head;
I have been faithful to thee, Cynara! in my fashion.

All night, upon my breast, I felt her warm heart beat;
Night long, within mine arms, in love and sleep she lay:
Surely the kisses of her bought, red mouth were sweet?
But I was desolate and sick of an old passion,
When I awoke, and found, the dawn was gray:
I have been faithful to thee, Cynara! in my fashion.

I have forgot much, Cynara! gone with the wind!
Flung roses, roses riotously with the throng;
Dancing, to put thy pale, lost lilies out of mind:
But I was desolate, and sick of an old passion;
Yea! desolate, because the dance was long:
I have been faithful to thee, Cynara! in my fashion.

I cried for madder music, and for stronger wine:
But, when the feast is finished, and the lamps expire,
Then falls thy shadow, Cynara! the night is thine!
And I am desolate, and sick of an old passion:
Yea! hungry for the lips of my desire:
I have been faithful to thee, Cynara! in my fashion.

From "*An Italian Garden*" by A. Mary
F. Robinson, (London, 1886.)

TORRENTS.

I KNOW *that if our lives could meet*
  Like torrents in a sudden tide,
Our souls should send their shining sheet
  Of waters far and wide.

But, ah! my dear, the springs of mine
  Have never yet begun to flow—
And yours, that were so full and fine,
  Ran dry so long ago!

From "A Book of Rhyme" by Augusta Webster, (London, 1881.)

NOT TO BE.

THE rose said *"Let but this long rain be past,*
  And I shall feel my sweetness in the sun
And pour its fullness into life at last."
   But when the rain was done,
But when dawn sparkled through unclouded air,
   She was not there.

The lark said "Let but winter be away,
  And blossoms come, and light, and I will soar,
And lose the earth, and be the voice of day."
   But when the snows were o'er,
But when spring broke in blueness overhead,
   The lark was dead.

And myriad roses made the garden glow, .
  And skylarks carolled all the summer long—
What lack of birds to sing and flowers to blow?
   Yet, ah, lost scent, lost song!
Poor empty rose, poor lark that never trilled!
   Dead unfulfilled!

From "Grass of Parnassus" by Andrew Lang, (London, 1888.)

GOOD-BYE.

K ISS *me, and say good-bye;*
Good-bye, there is no word to say but this,
Nor any lips left for my lips to kiss,
Nor any tears to shed, when these tears dry;
Kiss me, and say, good-bye.

Farewell, be glad, forget;
There is no need to say 'forget,' I know,
For youth is youth, and time will have it so,
And though your lips are pale, and your eyes wet,
Farewell, you must forget.

You shall bring home your sheaves,
Many, and heavy, and with blossoms twined
Of memories that go not out of mind;
Let this one sheaf be twined with poppy leaves
When you bring home your sheaves.

In garnered loves of thine,
The ripe good fruit of many hearts and years,
Somewhere let this lie, grey and salt with tears;
It grew too near the sea wind, and the brine
Of life, this love of mine.

This sheaf was spoiled in spring,
And over-long was green, and early sere,
And never gathered gold in the late year
From autumn suns, and moons of harvesting,
But failed in frosts of spring.

Yet was it thine, my sweet,
This love, though weak as young corn withered,
Whereof no man may gather and make bread;
Thine, though it never knew the summer heat;
Forget not quite, my sweet.

xlix

From "Poems" by Alice Meynell
(London, 1893.)

AFTER A PARTING.

Farewell has long been said; I have foregone thee;
  I never name thee even.
But how shall I learn virtues and yet shun thee?
  For thou art so near Heaven
That heavenward meditations pause upon thee.

Thou dost beset the path to every shrine;
  My trembling thoughts discern
Thy goodness in the good for which I pine;
  And if I turn from but one sin, I turn
Unto a smile of thine.

Now shall I trust thee apart
  Since all my growth tends to thee night and day—
To thee faith, hope, and art?
  Swift are the currents setting all one way;
They draw my life, my life, out of my heart.

From "Ailes D'Alouette" by F. W.
Bourdillon, (London, 1893.)

LIGHT.

THE night has a thousand eyes,
  And the day but one;
Yet the light of the bright world dies
  With the dying sun.

The mind has a thousand eyes,
  And the heart but one;
Yet the light of a whole life dies
  When love is done.

From "Silhouettes" by Arthur Symons,
(London, 1892.)

ALLA PASSERETTA BRUNA.

IF I bid you, you will come,
  If I bid you, you will go,
    You are mine, and so I take you
To my heart, your home ;
  Well, ah, well I know
    I shall not forsake you.

I shall always hold you fast,
  I shall never set you free,
    You are mine, and I possess you
Long as life shall last ;
  You will comfort me,
    I shall bless you.

I shall keep you as we keep
  Flowers for memory, hid away,
    Under many a newer token
Buried deep—
  Roses of a gaudier day,
    Rings and trinkets, bright and broken.

Other women I shall love,
  Fame and fortune I may win,
    But when fame and love forsake me
And the light is night above,
  You will let me in,
    You will take me.

From "Love is a Mist" (Anonymous),
(Oxford, 1892.)

MOTHER OF PEARL.

Not from all shells in Indian bays
Are pearls to win;
Nor hath the gentle heart always
A love within.

But where the pearl hath lain, the shells
Show yet the sheen;
And there's a soul-look that doth tell
Where love hath been.

From "A Book of Rhyme" by Augusta Webster, (London, 1881.)

WE TWO.

I.

We two that could not part are parted long;
   He in the far-off Heaven, and I to wait.
A fair world once, all blossom-time and song;
   But to be lonely tires, and I live late.
To think we two have not a word to change:
And one without the other here is strange!
   To think we two have nothing now to share:
   I wondering here, and he without me there!

II.

We two, we two! we still are linked and nigh:
   He could not have forgotten in any bliss;
Surely he feels my being yet; and I,
   I have no thought but seems some part of his.
Oh love gone out of reach of yearning eyes,
Our hearts can meet to gather-in replies:
   Oh love past touch of lip and clasp of hand,
   Thou canst not be too far to understand.

*From "Poems" by Paul Hamilton
Hayne, (Boston, 1882.)*

SWEETHEART, GOOD-BYE!

A SONG.

SWEEHEART, *good-bye! Our varied day
Is closing into twilight gray,
And up from bare, bleak wastes of sea
The north-wind rises mournfully;
A solemn prescience, strangely drear,
Doth haunt the shuddering twilight air;
It fills the earth, it chills the sky—
Sweetheart, good-bye!*

*Sweetheart, good-bye! Our joys are past,
And night with silence comes at last;
All things must end, yea,—even love—
Nor know we, if reborn above,
The heart-blooms of our earthly prime
Shall flower beyond these bounds of time.
"Ah! death alone is sure!" we cry—
Sweetheart, good-bye!*

*Sweetheart, good-bye! Through mists and tears
Pass the pale phantoms of our years,
Once bright with spring, or subtly strong
When summer's noontide thrilled with song;
Now wan, wild-eyed, forlornly bowed,
Each rayless as an autumn cloud
Fading on dull September's sky—
Sweetheart, good-bye!*

lv

Sweetheart, good-bye! The vapors rolled
Athwart yon distant, darkening wold
Are types of what our world doth know
Of tenderest loves of long ago;
And thus, when all is done and said,
Our life lived out, our passion dead,
What can their wavering record be
But tinted mists of memory?
Oh! clasp and kiss me ere we die—
        Sweetheart, good-bye!

From "Old World Idylls" by Austin Dobson, (London, 1885.)

BABETTE'S SONG.

O NCE *at the Angelus*
   (Ere I was dead,)
Angels all glorious
  . *Came to my Bed;—*
Angels in blue and white
  Crowned on the Head.

One was the Friend I left
  Stark in the Snow;
One was the Wife that died
  Long,—long ago;
One was the Love I lost . . .
  How could she know?

One had my Mother's eyes,
  Wistful and mild;
One had my Father's face;
  One was a Child:
All of them bent to me,—
  Bent down and smiled!

From "Poems" by Owen Meredith,
(Boston, 1872.)

ADIEU, MIGNONNE, MA BELLE.

ADIEU, *Mignonne, ma belle* . . . *when you are gone,*
  Vague thoughts of you will wander, searching love
Thro' this dim heart: thro' this dim room, Mignonne,
  *Vague fragrance from your hair and dress will
    move.*

How will you think of this poor heart to-morrow,
  This poor fond heart with all its joy in you?
Which you were fain to lean on, once, in sorrow,
  Though now you bid it such a light adieu.

You'll sing perchance . . . "I passed a night of dreams
  Once, in an old Inn's old worm-eaten bed,
Passing on life's highway. How strange it seems,
  That never more I there shall lean my head!"

Adieu, Mignonne, adieu Mignonne, ma belle!
  Ah little witch, our greeting was so gay,
Our love so painless, who'd have thought "Farewell!"
  Could ever be so sad a word to say?

I leave a thousand fond farewells with you: ·
  Some for your red wet lips, which were so sweet:
Some for your darling eyes, so dear, so blue:
  Some for your wicked, wanton little feet:

But for your little heart, not yet awake,—
  What can I leave your little heart, Mignonne?
It seems so fast asleep, I fear to break
  The poor thing's slumber. Let it still sleep on!

From "Primavera: Poems, by Four Authors,"
(Stephen Phillips), (Oxford, 1890.)

TO A LOST LOVE.

I CANNOT *look upon thy grave,*
  Though there the rose is sweet :
Better to bear the long wave wash
  These wastes about my feet!

Shall I take comfort ? Dost thou live
  A spirit, though afar,
With a deep hush about thee, like
  The stillness round a star ?

Oh, thou art cold! In that high sphere
  Thou art a thing apart,
Losing in saner happiness
  This madness of the heart.

And yet, at times, thou still shalt feel
  A passing breath, a pain ;
Disturb'd, as though a door in heaven
  Had oped and closed again.

And thou shalt shiver, while the hymns,
  The solemn hymns, shall cease ;
A moment half remember me :
  Then turn away to peace.

But oh, for evermore thy look,
  Thy laugh, thy charm, thy tone,
Thy sweet and wayward earthliness,
  Dear trivial things, are gone!

Therefore I look not on thy grave,
  Though there the rose is sweet ;
But rather bear the loud wave wash
  These wastes about my feet.

From "Tares" (Anonymous),
(London, 1884.)

HERBSTLIED.

FAREWELL, *my love, I love so well!*
  My sweetheart, lost as soon as won!
Sweet summer idyll, scarce begun—
    Farewell!

Good-bye brown fields, and wind-swept skies,
With mellow sunset all aglow:
Unto the bitter north I go—
    Good-bye!

Ah me, dear heart, Auf Wiederseh'n!
Surely one day we'll meet again;
And lest our hope relinquished be,
This watchword give Mnemosyne—
    "Auf Wiederseh'n!"

*From "Songs of Life and Death" by
John Payne, (London, 1884.)*

SONGS' END.

I.

THE chime of a bell of gold
  That flutters across the air,
The sound of a singing of old,
The end of a tale that is told,
  Of a melody strange and fair,
  Of a joy that has grown despair:

II.

For the things that have been for me
  I shall never have them again;
The skies and the purple sea,
And day like a melody,
  And night like a silver rain
  Of stars on forest and plain.

III.

They are shut, the gates of the day;
  The night has fallen on me:
My life is a lightless way;
I sing yet, while as I may!
  Some day I shall cease, maybe:
  I shall live on yet, you will see.

.

From "Lyrics and Ballads" by Margaret
L. Woods, (London, 1889.)

L'ENVOI.

*Like the wreath the poet sent
    To the lady of old time,
Roses that were discontent
    With their brief unhonoured prime,
    Crown he hoped she might endow
    With the beauty of her brow;
Even so for you I blent,
Send to you my wreath of rhyme.*

*These alas! be blooms less bright,
    Faded buds that never blew,
Darkling thoughts that seek the light—
    Let them find it finding you.
    Bid these petals pale unfold
    On your heart their hearts of gold,
Sweetness for your sole delight,
Love for odour, tears for dew.*

From "Beside Dead Fires"
(*Anonymous.*)

"WHEN FINIS COMES."

SWEETHEART, 'tis true stars rise and set,
  And all fair seasons cease to be,
  The sunlight fades from off the sea,
And wintry winds our rose leaves fret;
Yet past the reach of barren hours
Across the years are shining yet
Your face and eyes—can I forget
Their lovely light that shines on me?
  Nay, sweet, these change not, these abide
Beyond the stress of Time and Tide,
Across the years in Youth's fair clime
Live all lost loves and all dead flowers,—
The Land of Memory knows no Time.

Here Ends Songs of Adieu;
A Little Book of Finalé and
Farewell.